Hooey Higgins

and the

Tremendous
Trousers

For Lucy Earley
S.V.

For Lorenzo
E.D.

HOOEY HIGGINS
and the
tremendous
trousers

STEVE VOAKE
illustrated by Emma Dodson

WALKER
BOOKS

This is a work of fiction. Names, characters, places and incidents are either the product of the author's imagination or, if real, used fictitiously. All statements, activities, stunts, descriptions, information and material of any other kind contained herein are included for entertainment purposes only and should not be relied on for accuracy or replicated as they may result in injury.

First published 2010 by Walker Books Ltd
87 Vauxhall Walk, London SE11 5HJ

2 4 6 8 10 9 7 5 3 1

Text © 2010 Steve Voake
Illustrations © 2010 Emma Dodson

The right of Steve Voake and Emma Dodson to be identified as author and illustrator respectively of this work has been asserted by them in accordance with the Copyright, Designs and Patents Act 1988

This book has been typeset in StempelSchneidler and EDodson

Printed and bound in Great Britain
by Clays Ltd, St Ives plc

British Library Cataloguing in Publication Data:
a catalogue record for this book is available from the British Library

ISBN 978-1-4063-2236-1

www.walker.co.uk

CONTENTS

BANANA
BOG ROLLS

"HEALTH AND SAFETY, HEALTH AND SAFETY!" shouted Miss Troutson, clapping her hands together and peering over the top of her glasses. "What did I say about Health and Safety?"

Hooey Higgins stopped what he was doing and looked around. The whole class had stopped at the same time and it was like a freeze-frame from a horror movie:

Yasmin Boothroyd had a hammer raised above her head, Ricky Mears was holding a nail and a piece of wood in front of his face and

Twig appeared to be trying to saw his legs in half.

Meanwhile, on
the far side of
the classroom,
Robbie Blunt
had his hands
in the air and
Basbo Wilkins
was squinting
at him over
the top of a
stapler.

"I want everyone
to stop what
they're doing
and come and
sit on the carpet

IMMEDIATELY.

Hooey was quite pleased in a way. He'd started out with high hopes for his model of a big wheel, but the cheese carton kept falling off the end of the pencil and crushing all the little Plasticine customers. Which, he had to admit, wasn't healthy or safe.

Hooey put down his scissors and sat next to Twig, who had actually been sawing through toilet roll tubes and was now using one of them as a telescope.

LAND AHOY! he shouted,

LAND AHOY!

and kept shouting it until Miss Troutson leaned over and took the tube away.

"All right," she said when everyone was settled. "Can anyone tell me what our theme was in science last week? Yasmin?"

"STAYING HEALTHY, STAYING SAFE," said Yasmin.

"Very good, Yasmin. So why do you think I stopped everyone just now?"

"Because people weren't being Healthy or Safe," said Twig. "They were being Unhealthy and Dangerous." He looked at Basbo. "With staplers mainly."

"That is correct," said Miss Troutson, as Basbo glared back at Twig. "So your homework this weekend is to come up with a design for something that will make the world a safer place."

"Boring," said Basbo, aiming the stapler at Twig. Twig panicked, jerked his head back and banged it on the filing cabinet.

"That is *not* the attitude," said Miss Troutson, holding one hand out for the stapler while patting Twig sympathetically with the other. "But I thought a few of you might feel that way.

Which is why I have spoken to the owner
of the fairground and he has agreed to give
a prize to the person who presents the best
safety design in class assembly on Monday."

"Ooh," said Twig, forgetting his injuries.
"Is it candyfloss?"

"Better than that," said Miss Troutson.
"The winner will get free tickets to the fair."

*   *   *

Outside, the day was heavy with heat and sunshine. Infants monkeyed around in the hedges, Basbo demonstrated wrestling moves on Ricky Mears, and Samantha Curbitt ran rings around the Watson twins before flicking the ball up and scoring her third hat trick.

"She's an angel," said Twig, smiling dreamily. "An angel sent from heaven."

"You shouldn't talk about Basbo like that," said Hooey. "He might hear you."

They watched as Basbo flipped Ricky Mears over his head and dumped him in the shrubbery.

"I think he actually wants to kill me," said Twig. "Did you see his face when he aimed the stapler at me?"

"He always looks like that," said Hooey. "Probably just concentrating."

"Yeah, on stapling my head to the wall."

"Never mind that," said Hooey. "Just think about those free tickets. They've got our name on them, Twiggy-boy."

"Maybe we could design something for the little hedge-monkeys," said Twig, watching the infants make their dens in the hedges at the bottom of the field. "Something to keep them safe."

"But hedges aren't dangerous, Twig," said Hooey.

"They are if you put the right dog in there," said Twig. "There's one round our way that'll go for anything. He's a complete nutmeg."

"Twig, you're grasping at straws," said Hooey. "Maybe we should just try and get some ideas at the fair tonight."

"OK," said Twig. "I haven't got any money though. I spent it all on toilet paper."

"*Toilet* paper?"

"Yeah. I needed the rolls for my model of the water chute."

"So what happened to the paper?"

"I wrapped it round some bananas. I thought it could be like a surprise treat for people when they finish the roll. You know: *Oooh, a banana!* Like that."

"It's a bit weird, Twig," said Hooey. "But quite healthy, I suppose. It could help people with their five portions a day."

"That could be our design!" said Twig. "BANANA BOG ROLLS! We could write to the Prime Minister and everything."

Hooey imagined the look on the Prime Minister's face when he opened his post and found a banana wrapped in toilet paper. "Maybe we'll come back to that one," he said.

At that moment, Hooey's brother Will arrived carrying his sandwich box in one hand and a notebook in the other. On the front of the notebook he had written: **My Decimal Calculations by Will Higgins.**

"Ooh, look!" cried Twig, pointing at the cover. "It's `Danny the Decimal Point`!"

"It's chocolate actually," said Will, scratching it off with his thumbnail. "And anyway, decimals aren't called Danny."

"They are in my maths group," said Twig. "`Danny the Decimal Point` and `Sammy Subtraction`. They live together in `Maths Mansion` with `Molly Multiplication` and `Davina Division`."

"I think Will's doing more complicated stuff than that," said Hooey. "Show him, Will."

"OK, listen to this," said Will, flicking

through the pages. "I worked out that the average number of digestive biscuits eaten by people in this school is 1.97 a day."

Twig pressed his hands to his cheeks with excitement. "1 *point* 97!" he said. "Wow."

"Wait," said Will. "There's more." He opened his lunch box and produced a digestive biscuit from beneath his tuna-fish sandwiches. "I worked out that if you stacked up all the biscuits for the next seventy years, the pile would stretch past Mount Everest and all the way into space."

"No *way*!" said Twig. "No wayno wayno *way*!"

Will held up his notebook. "Check it out, Twig. The pictures don't lie."

Hooey peered over Twig's shoulder and saw that Will had drawn a diagram showing lots of kids lying on their backs, with packets of digestive biscuits strewn all around them. Another picture showed a snow-topped mountain with a pile of biscuits stretching past it into space. Next to it was a huge tower of children, balancing on each other's shoulders. The boy at the top was wearing a helmet and adding more digestives to the pile.

"They just hand 'em up," said Will. "Takes roughly 9.7 hours per biscuit."

"Have you got any *actual* photos?" asked Twig hopefully.

"Not yet," said Will. "But it's only a matter of time, Twig. It's only a matter of time."

Hooey cleared his throat. "Umm, Will, leaving the digestives to one side for a moment, can you help us with our project? We need to design something safe."

"Safe?" Will frowned. "What kind of safe?"

"The kind that will win us free tickets to the fair. Miss Troutson's giving them away to the winners of the best safety design. Also, Twig needs some money and we think Basbo wants to kill him."

Twig went slightly pale at the mention of this last bit, but Will just nodded and took a fresh pencil from his pocket.

"What are you thinking, Will?" asked Hooey.

Will licked the end of his pencil and opened his notebook.

"I'm thinking trousers," he said.

A BET WITH BASBO

"Trousers?" said Twig.

"*Interesting,*" said Hooey.

"The way I see it," said Will, "there are three separate tasks." He took his notebook and wrote:

1.   Design something to do with safety.

2.   Get Twig some money.

3.   Stop Basbo killing Twig.

He turned it round to show Hooey and Twig.

"Yep," said Hooey. "Reckon that about covers it."

Will beckoned Hooey over and whispered in his ear. Hooey listened. Then he smiled.

"What?" said Twig. "What's he saying?"

"Don't worry," said Hooey. "Will's just going to talk to a few people over there. In the meantime, we need to go and talk to someone else."

"See you by the hedge," said Will, tucking his pencil in his top pocket.

As Will walked across to where Samantha was heading in goal number ten, Hooey took Twig by the elbow and walked him across the field.

"I don't get it," said Twig. "Where are we going?"

"To see a friend of yours," said Hooey.

In the middle of the field, Basbo was spinning Johnny Bertram round above his head.

WOaaaah!

waaaay!

Johnny was yelling, his voice becoming softer as he spun away and louder when he spun back again.

Twig looked at Hooey. "I'm going to die, aren't I?"

"Relax," said Hooey. "No one's going to die. We're just going to have a chat, that's all."

"I can't chat with anyone," said Twig, "if I haven't got a head."

When Basbo saw them, he let go of Johnny Bertram, who sailed off across the grass like a tiny meteorite. He bounced twice, got up and waved, then staggered off towards the monkey bars.

"See?" said Hooey. "Not a scratch on him."

Basbo stared at them for a few moments, then pointed at Twig with a short, stubby finger. "You bunky little bongaweed," he said. "You grizzled me up to Troutson, didn't ya? You opened your flappy-trap and mazzed me up like a minky."

Twig gulped loudly, but Hooey stepped forward and held up his finger. "Um, if I could just interrupt you for a second there, Baz?"

Basbo scrunched up his fists like a couple of cannonballs and scowled so that his eyebrows met in the middle.

"Ya got five seconds, finklewit. I ain't got time for wazzin' with a wozzer like you."

"No, of course you haven't," said Hooey. "But the thing is, I was just having a disagreement with my brother Will over there and I need your help to settle it once and for all."

Basbo frowned. "You want me to fwap him in the bongers?"

"Not really, no," said Hooey hurriedly. "It's just he reckons that Twig here can beat you in a staring contest—"

"What?" said Twig, his voice going up an octave. "When did he—"

"But I said," continued Hooey, "that there's no way Twig could beat you in a million years. I said you could out-stare anyone, anytime, no question about it."

Basbo grabbed Twig by the shirt and pulled him up until their noses were nearly touching. "Think you can beat me, do ya, y'little frambit?"

"No!" squeaked Twig. "I never—"

"Don't worry," said Hooey stepping between them and straightening out Twig's shirt. "When my brother gets these ideas in his head, there's just no stopping him."

He glanced across the field and saw that Will was standing by the hedge with a crowd of people around him. "Why don't you show him, Bazzer? Show him once and for all who's the best starer in Shrimpton-on-Sea!"

Hooey's words seemed to make quite an impression on Basbo. It was as if the leader of the OLYMPIC STARING TEAM had suddenly called to say that their staring champion had unexpectedly been taken ill, and would he, Basbo, mind taking his place? Basbo clenched his fists, his eyes lit up and he nodded aggressively as if this was the moment he had been waiting for all his life.

"Right, y'little wozzers," he said.

*   *   *

When they reached the other side of the field, Will was standing by the hedge holding a clipboard. A crowd of children and dinner ladies had gathered around him, chattering excitedly.

"Ah, Mr Bazzer," he said as if he had invited Basbo over for a job interview. "So glad you could come." He turned to Twig. "And you are?"

"I'm Twig," said Twig. "As you already know."

Will nodded and made a note on his clipboard. "Just checking for the record, Twig."

Twig looked bewildered, as if he was having one of those dreams where meerkats ride bicycles and juggle with melons.

Basbo glared at Will. "I hear you reckon this Twiglet's a better starer than me."

Will pushed his glasses back up his nose and nodded. "This is true," he said, "but as a scientist I am willing to be proved wrong. In fact," he added, "if it turns out that you are better at staring, I will give you twenty pence."

Basbo frowned. "TWENNY PENCE?"

Will took out a silver twenty pence piece and held it up between finger and thumb. "Twenty pence," he said. "In cash."

Basbo couldn't have looked more surprised if Will had pulled a rabbit from a hat and made it sing the theme tune from *Star Wars*. "Right," he said. "You're on."

Will turned to Hooey. "If you would like to show the contestants to their seats, then we can begin."

A hush fell over the crowd and Hooey began to get nervous. Will was usually pretty good at working stuff out, but this was definitely his most ambitious plan yet. If it all went wrong, there was a good chance Basbo would grab all three of them and stuff their heads down the nearest toilet.

"Now then, Bazzer," he said, feeling like a presenter on a daytime reality show, "if you'd like to come and sit over here, then we can—no, not there, just here, that's it, thank you."

34

"Are you MAD?" hissed Twig in a panicky voice as Basbo sat on the grassy mound opposite him. Basbo was making soft growly noises, like a bad-tempered dog who has heard a rumour that the postman is coming. All around them, the crowd of children and dinner ladies waited patiently for things to get started. Some of the infants at the back had even climbed onto the shoulders of the older ones to get a better view.

Hooey patted Twig on the back. "All set, champ?"

"Hooey, I don't know what you're trying to do," said Twig nervously, "but there's no way I'm going to win this. Basbo could stare his way through a brick wall."

"You don't need to win," whispered Hooey. *"That's the beauty of it all."*

As he stepped forward and clapped his hands together like a mini Miss Troutson, Hooey realized that he was actually quite enjoying himself. "OK!" he shouted. "IS EVERYONE READY?"

"YAY!" cried the crowd.

TROUSER TROUBLE

Basbo leaned forward and stared until his eyes bulged like soft-boiled eggs.

Twig rested his hands on his knees and raised his eyebrows until they disappeared under his fringe.

"OOOOH!" went the crowd.

"BAS-BO, BAS-BO!" chanted one side.

"TWIG-LET, TWIG-LET!" chanted the other.

Hooey turned to Will. "This is going quite well," he said. "D'you think he could win?"

"Who cares?" said Will. "All that matters is trousers."

"BAS-BO, BAS-BO!"

"TWIG-LET, TWIG-LET!"

"BAS-BO, BAS-BO!"

"TWIG-LET, TWIG-LET!"

"BAS-BO!"

"TWIG-LET!"

"BAS-BO!"

"TWIG-LET!"

"BAS-BO, BAS-BO!"

"TWIG-LET, TWIG-LET!"

Basbo stared.
The crowd
fell silent.
Twig stared.
The crowd held
their breath.
Basbo stared
harder.
Twig stared back
and then he …

BLINKED!

"Awwwwwww!"
went the crowd.

"GET IN THERE!"
shouted Basbo, clasping
his hands above his head as
everyone cheered. He walked
over to Will and held out his
hand. "Twenny pence, y'little
frarpsichord!"

"Sure thing," said Will, handing over
the money with a flourish. "You won it
fair and square."

"That was great, Basbo," said Hooey.
"But some people reckon it was just a fluke.
Maybe you should do it again, just to prove
that you're the absolute total champion."

"Hooey's right," agreed Will. "And I tell you what, if you do it again, I'll throw in another twenty pence."

Basbo's eyes lit up like two cracked headlamps. "Easy money," he growled, sitting on the grass tussock and cracking his knuckles. "Come on, Twiglet, let's see if ya got any more stares in yer stash."

Twig crossed his legs, shut his eyes and held his hands out in front of him, palms upwards. He touched the thumb and forefinger of each hand together and breathed slowly in and out.

"What's up, Twig?" asked Hooey.

"Shh!" said Twig. "I'm meditating."

"Well do it with your eyes open," said Hooey. "They're all waiting for the second stare-off. Including *Samantha*."

Twig opened one eye and looked at him. "Samantha? Was that her doing the **TWIGLET-TWIGLET** thing?"

"Yup. Her and a couple of dinner ladies. Now come on, Twig. Big effort, eh?"

"Right," said Twig, opening his other eye. "I'm ready."

"**HE'S READY!**" shouted Hooey.

"**HE'S READY!**" cheered the crowd.

"**AND ... STARE!**" said Hooey.

The crowd went silent.

Basbo stared.

Twig stared back.

Basbo stared some more.

Twig stared back.

Then Basbo began to twitch.

"**EH?**" went the crowd.

Twig kept staring.

Basbo started to itch and scratch.

"**HUH?**" went the crowd.

Will winked at Hooey. "And three, two, one…" he said.

"**YOWCH!**" yelled Basbo, jumping up and clutching his trousers. "**YOW-OW-OW-OW-OWCH!**"

As the crowd gasped, Basbo kicked off his shoes, pulled down his trousers and ran across the field as if his pants were on fire, his cries fading as he leapt down the steps and disappeared into the toilets.

"YAY!" yelled the crowd. "TROUSERS OFF! TROUSERS OFF! TROUSERS OFF! TROUSERS OFF!"

The dinner ladies began jumping up and down chanting, "TROUSERS OFF! TROUSERS OFF! TROUSERS OFF! TROUSERS OFF!"

...until the chief dinner lady remembered they weren't supposed to shout things like that and made them all shush up.

As the crowd began to disperse, Hooey turned to see that Twig was sitting with his eyes wide open, still staring at the spot where Basbo had been.

"You can stop now, Twig," said Hooey, waving a hand in front of his face. "Basbo's gone."

Twig looked up at Hooey and blinked. "I had the strangest dream," he said. "People were shouting TROUSERS! and Basbo wasn't wearing any."

"That was no dream, Twig," said Hooey. "That was the real deal."

Twig shook his head. "But why? How? And what about the staring contest?"

"That was just a way of getting Basbo to sit in the same spot for long enough."

Twig looked at Hooey as if he was completely mad. "Why would you want him to do that?"

"Because Will made a bet, that's why."

"I know. He bet Basbo couldn't out-stare me. But he was wrong, wasn't he? So instead of making money, he's lost twenty pence." Twig sighed. "And I thought Will was supposed to be the smart one."

Hooey grinned. "Take a look over there, Twig." He pointed to a corner of the field where Will was standing with his hands cupped in front of him. A large crowd of children and dinner ladies were queuing up to give him money.

"What's he doing?" asked Twig.

"Collecting bets."

"But he lost."

"Oh he lost the staring one. But he also bet he could get Basbo to take his trousers off – and that one is *definitely* paying off."

Twig's eyes widened. "Will bet that?"

"Yup."

The corners of Twig's mouth began to turn up in the faintest of smiles. "No *way*! No wayno wayno way!"

They turned to look at Will who appeared to be walking awkwardly, his legs bowing out like a cowboy who has been too long in the saddle. But as he got closer the reason became clear: his pockets were bulging with coins.

"Shirt, Twig," said Hooey.

Twig held out his shirt and Will emptied fistfuls of coins into it. As Twig stared open-mouthed at the pile of money, Will opened his notebook, took out his pen and studied his list.

"So let's see here:

Get Twig some money. Check.

Stop Basbo killing Twig. Check.

Design something to do with safety.
Still to do."

Will clicked the top of his pen and put it back in his pocket. "Oh well. Two out of three's not bad."

"I don't get it," said Twig. "How did you get Basbo to take his trousers off?"

"Easy," said Will. "All we had to do was sit him on an ants' nest."

Twig frowned. He stared at the mound of earth where Basbo had been sitting. He looked at Will. Then, very slowly, he started to smile.

"I think he's got it," said Hooey.

"Right," said Will. "I'm off to the library to design some insect-proof trousers. I think they could be the next big thing."

"Incredible," said Twig when Will had gone. "How come he's so brainy?"

"Must be all those tuna-fish sandwiches he eats," said Hooey.

"I prefer crackers," said Twig. "Crackers and nuts."

Hooey nodded.

DANGER ON THE DODGEMS

As Hooey sat with Twig at the top of the big wheel, swinging the seat and looking down at the bright lights of the fair, a thought occurred to him. "You know what would be amazing?" he said.

"Ooh, hang on, I know this," said Twig. "Your head exploding. Sticking a toffee apple up your nose."

"Eee ... yes," agreed Hooey, studying his toffee apple at arm's length. "Both those things *would* be amazing. But actually I was thinking how great it would be to have some special trousers."

Twig nodded enthusiastically. "Who wouldn't want a pair of those?"

"They wouldn't be just for ants either," Hooey went on. "They could protect you against loads of other stuff too."

"Tremendous!" said Twig.

Hooey stared at him. "That's what we should call them, Twig," he said. "TREMENDOUS TROUSERS. Or TREMTROOS for short."

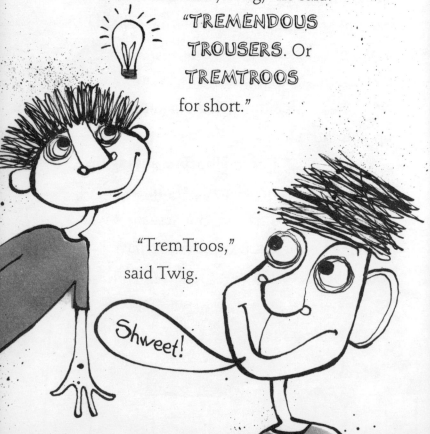

"TremTroos," said Twig.

Shweet!

Until now, TremTroos were not something Hooey had ever considered. But as he looked up at the bright lights of the big wheel, he realized that sometimes the simplest ideas are the best.

"The problem is," he said, "we need to work out how to make them before class assembly on Monday."

"Problem shmoblem," said Twig. "My Uncle Ernie says a problem is just another name for an opportunity."

"Is that the same Uncle Ernie who got his leg bitten off by a crocodile?"

"Not all of it. Just a bit off the end."

"And what opportunities did that give him?"

"He got to see the film *Beverly Hills Chihuahua* on the flight home. Which he'd have missed if he'd stayed in Florida."

"Did he enjoy it?"

"Not really. He doesn't like dogs." Twig paused for a moment. "Or crocodiles."

"See, now that's because he wasn't wearing TremTroos," said Hooey. "The world's crying out for them, Twig. We just need to think hard."

"Thinking gives me a headache," said Twig. "Can't we get Will to do it for us?"

When they got off the big wheel, Will was waiting for them at the bottom.

"We've been giving the trouser thing some thought," Hooey told him. "Instead of just insect-proof ones, you could have trousers that protect you against other stuff too. Like crocodiles."

"Or Basbo," said Twig.

"We thought we'd call them TREMTROOS," said Hooey.

Will nodded. "Yep. Makes sense."

Hooey noticed Will was holding a diagram of himself standing at the coconut shy. He had drawn an arrow going from his hand to a coconut and there were lots of numbers written next to it.

"What are those?" asked Hooey.

"They're my calculations," Will explained. He licked his finger and held it up in the air. "Feel that breeze?"

"No."

"Well there is one. And by my calculations, it's moving at about one kilometre per hour. You know what that means, don't you?"

"We'll stay nice and cool?" suggested Twig.

"No," said Will. "It means it's going to play havoc with my shots. So I'm going to throw the ball slightly to the left, then the wind will blow it back on course and knock the coconut off."

"I didn't know you liked throwing stuff at coconuts," said Twig.

"I don't," said Will. "But if you win you get to choose a colouring pack with fifty felt pens in it. It's like a rainbow, but with 7.14 times as many colours."

"7 *point* 14!" said Twig. "Shweet!"

"ROLL UP, ROLL UP, ROLL UP!" shouted the man on the coconut shy. "Three balls for a pound."

Will took another look at his drawing, then handed it to Hooey and picked up the first ball. Closing one eye, he drew his arm back and threw the ball as hard as he could. It thumped into a teddy bear, which slumped forwards and fell off the shelf as if it had been shot.

"Hmm, the wind's picked up," said Will. He turned slightly so that his left shoulder was facing forward. This time the ball zoomed off to the right of the middle coconut and thwacked into the straw bales at the back.

"Maybe you should try aiming at the coconuts," said Twig.

"Maybe we should just leave Will to concentrate," said Hooey.

After stopping for Twig to buy some candyfloss, they stood by the Dodgems and watched the cars flying around the circuit.

"I'm not going on those," said Hooey, shaking his head. "Just look at them. I've never seen such terrible drivers."

Twig peered out from behind his candyfloss. "You're joking, right?"

Hooey grinned. "Course I'm joking."

As the cars came to a halt, he took a bite from his toffee apple and nudged Twig with his elbow. "C'mon, Twig. Let's go and have an accident."

"Ooh, I *love* candyfloss," said Twig, sliding into the passenger seat next to Hooey. "It's like eating an ickle cloud."

"Yeah, well you might want to try hiding behind it," said Hooey, "'cos Basbo's driving the car over there."

Twig turned pale as he looked at the car on the other side of the circuit. Basbo was crammed into his seat like a troll in a training shoe and his spiky hair stuck up as if it was trying to suck sparks from the electric grid.

"He's not wearing his seatbelt," said Twig. "Maybe I should go and tell him."

"Why?"

"Health and Safety. It's dangerous."

"Not as dangerous as you telling him that it's dangerous. Look at him. He's like a lion watching wildebeest. Just waiting to move in for the kill."

"Thanks Hooey," said Twig. "That makes me feel a lot better."

"I know something that *will* make you feel better," said Hooey. "I've just seen Samantha Curbitt getting into a car over there."

"**Yowzee**," said Twig, quickly smoothing his hair down. "How do I look?"

"Like a chimp who's found some candyfloss," said Hooey. He put his foot down, turned the wheel and spun the car out into the centre of the circuit.

"OK, here she comes," said Twig. "Think I'll just act casual."

As they drew alongside each other, he put his elbow on the edge of the car, leaned out and smiled. "Hello Samantha," he said. "You're a good driver."

"Get lost, NUMPTY," said Samantha.

"Can't, I'm afraid," said Twig. "My driver here knows these roads like the back of his hand."

He was still trying to think of something
else to say when there was a huge thump,
the car shot sideways and Twig flew head
first into the footwell.

"Take that, y'little weenburgers!"
shouted Basbo.

As Hooey rescued the toffee apple
from his lap, Twig
emerged from the
footwell with his
face covered in
candyfloss.

Hooey grinned.
"I see the airbag
works then."

"Very funny," said
Twig, scraping lumps of candyfloss
off his face. He was just climbing back into
his seat when there was another thump and
the car spun around in a circle.

"**Way-hey!**" shouted Hooey, clutching his toffee apple and wrestling with the steering wheel. "We're under attack!"

"That was Samantha!" cried Twig excitedly. "Come on, Hooey. Let's get after her!"

Hooey pressed his foot down on the accelerator, but as they gathered speed he noticed that Basbo's car was heading straight for them.

"**Uh-oh**," whimpered Twig, clamping his hands over his eyes. "HEALTH AND SAFETY, HEALTH AND SAFETY!"

Seconds before impact, Samantha
Curbitt's car rammed into the back of Basbo
and a fourth car rammed into the back of
Hooey. As the cars smashed into each other,
the crunch of bumpers was so loud it sent
all the pigeons on the roof of the ghost
train squawking into the air.

Luckily for Twig and Hooey,
they were both wearing their seatbelts.
Unluckily for Basbo, he wasn't.

All around the steps of the Dodgems, people heard the crash and turned to see Basbo flying out of his seat. Many were surprised by the fact that such a large boy could soar through the air with such speed and grace, even managing to flap his arms a couple of times along the way.

Some said that if there had been more space, he might have been the first person ever to fly across Shrimpton unaided. But unfortunately for Basbo, space was the one thing he didn't have.

In the control booth, Dave the Dodgems looked up to see what appeared to be an enormous seagull heading straight for him.

"What the—?" he said, and then a large boy in a football top slammed into the window, sending his mug of tea splooshing up the wall over his favourite picture of Kylie Minogue.

Dave watched in horror as the boy slid down the glass with a faint squeaking sound. "OI!" he shouted, pointing at a sign which said: PLEASE DO NOT DISTRACT THE OPERATOR. "Can't you read?!"

"Come on," said Hooey as Basbo staggered to his feet. "I think we should probably be going."

When they found Will a few minutes later, he was clutching a large pack of felt pens.

"Funniest thing just happened," he said.

"I was throwing my last ball when there was this massive bang and then something came zinging past my left ear. It hit the coconut, ricocheted off and whacked the man in the you-know-wheres. He was so shocked he just staggered about for a bit and then gave me these."

"Shweet!" said Twig.

"This thing that flew past your ear," said Hooey thoughtfully. "It wasn't red and shiny, was it?"

Will nodded. "I think so. Did you see it too?"

"No," said Hooey with a grin. "But that explains where my toffee apple went."

TREMENDOUS
TROUSERS

"The world is a dangerous place," said Hooey as they walked Dingbat along the seafront the next morning. "What with flying toffee apples and all the rest of it."

"Don't forget flying Basbos," said Twig.

"What we need," said Hooey, "is a pair of trousers that will save us from all these things. And we need them by Monday."

"It's a tall order," said Will. "No doubt about it."

They stopped outside DEREK DANSON'S DELICIOUS DELICACIES and peered in through the window. Mr Danson had built a model of a big wheel from a construction kit and as it turned around, little chocolate truffles swung about in their seats. Above it was a sign which said:

DEREK DANSON WELCOMES THE FUNFAIR TO SHRIMPTON-ON-SEA

"That is one classy piece of engineering," said Will. "Maybe Mr Danson will be able to give us some ideas."

The doorbell dinged as they walked into the shop and Mr Danson looked up from the counter. "Ah, bonjour my little chocolatiers," he said. "What can I get for you this morning? Truffles from Transylvania? Caramels from Canada?"

"Just the usual please, Mr Danson," said Hooey, placing some change on the counter. "Three Crunchies and a bag of toffee bonbons."

"An excellent choice if I may say so," said Mr Danson, handing Hooey the Crunchies. "Or perhaps I should say a bon choice, eh? Bonbon!" He chuckled to himself and reached down the jar.

As Mr Danson was putting the sweets in a bag, Hooey noticed Dingbat sniffing at some empty boxes behind the counter.

"Mr Danson," he said, "have you finished with those boxes?"

"Indeed I have," said Mr Danson. "That was my delivery of diet cola. Half the calories means twice the chocolate."

He handed Hooey the toffee bonbons. "You want the boxes?"

"Not really," said Hooey, "but I wouldn't mind the stuff that's in them."

Mr Danson pulled out a handful of bubble wrap. "This?"

Hooey nodded. "We need to make some special trousers, you see. By Monday."

"Ah, now I understand," said Mr Danson, tapping the side of his nose. "You are designers, dreamers. Artists like myself, yes?"

"Well, er—"

"Yes, yes! Of course you are! People like us are always on the lookout for the new, the fashionable, the cutting edge! Just as I work magic with *le chocolat*, so you will work your magic with … trousers. Am I right?"

"**YES!**" cried Twig, suddenly overcome.
"We will make MAGICAL trousers! We will
bring **TREMTROOS** to the waiting world!"

Dingbat barked excitedly and began
running round in circles. Hooey raised an
eyebrow. "Twig," he said, "just help me get
the bubble wrap, will you?"

"Sorry," said Twig. "I don't know what
came over me."

As they scooped up armfuls of bubble
wrap, Hooey noticed Will staring into space.
"You OK there, Will?" he asked.

"Shhh!" whispered Mr Danson, putting a
finger to his lips. "I think he is dreaming
of your trousers."

"Diet cola…" mumbled Will,
putting his roll of wallpaper
onto the counter. "Of
course, of *course*."

He unrolled the paper, took a pencil from his pocket and began scribbling.

"Come on, Will," said Hooey opening the door. "We need this done before Monday."

"You go ahead," said Will. "I've still got some thinking to do."

"D'you think he's all right?" asked Twig as they walked up the road to Hooey's house.

"He's planning something," said Hooey. "You know what it's like when you suddenly get an idea."

"Nope," said Twig. "Can't say I do."

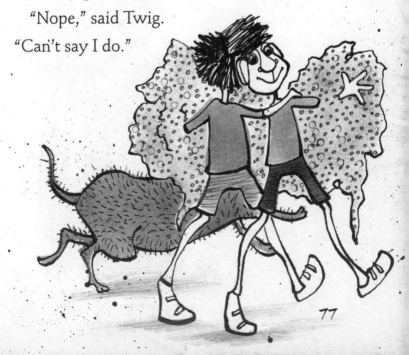

77

When they got home, Grandpa was making toast and Grandma was in the lounge shouting, "Get down, Vera! Get *down* on that canvas!"

"Is Grandma OK?" asked Hooey.

"She's fine," said Grandpa. "She's boxing on the Nintendo Wii with Mrs Jenkins."

Hooey peered round the corner to see Grandma and Mrs Jenkins clutching Nintendo controllers. They were both staring at the screen and flailing their arms about.

"Hello dears," called Grandma as Dingbat barked and thumped his tail on the floor. "I'm just opening up a can of SMACKY-PUNCH for Vera."

"OH YEAH?" shouted Vera. "Well take that! And that! And *that*!"

"I'll say one thing for your gran," said Twig as they sat at the kitchen table. "She's got a mean left hook."

"You should see her on Pro Wrestling," said Grandpa. "No one can get near her."

"Grandpa," said Hooey, "I don't suppose you've got any spare trousers?"

Grandpa patted his pockets. "Fresh out, I'm afraid. But I can check upstairs if you like. What d'you need them for?"

"We need to make some special ones," said Hooey. "For Emergency Purposes."

"I see," said Grandpa, taking a bite of toast and feeding the rest to Dingbat. "What kind of emergencies did you have in mind?"

"Oh you know," said Twig, "fairground accidents, flying toffee apples, that kind of thing."

Grandpa nodded. "Well you can never be too careful. Although I think my trousers might be a bit on the roomy side."

"They're not for me," said Hooey. "They're for Twig."

"**Eh?**" said Twig. "Why me?"

"Because they're going to need very special testing," said Hooey. "And *you* are a Very Special Tester."

Twig smiled. "I'm a Special Tester," he said.

"What we need is ex*pandable* trousers," said Hooey. "Big, stretchy, expandable ones."

Grandpa thought for a moment. "I know the very thing," he said and disappeared out the back.

"Big stretchy expandable ones?" said Twig. "What for?"

"Three reasons," said Hooey. "One: You need to feel comfortable. Two: You need to look normal. And three: We need to stuff a load of bubble wrap down your trousers."

"How's having bubble wrap down my trousers going to make me look normal?" asked Twig.

"I'm not going to lie to you, Twig," said Hooey. "It's going to be tricky. But I'm confident we can do it."

"We?" said Twig. "You're not the one who has to wear them."

"How about these?" asked Grandpa as he walked back into the kitchen. "Grandma doesn't wear them much now she's got the Nintendo."

Hooey and Twig stared at the huge pair of bright yellow tracksuit bottoms that Grandpa was holding up.

"Perfect," said Hooey.

Twig looked at Hooey and then back at the trousers again.

"You have *got* to be kidding."

*   *   *

The Pinkertons, who lived next door, were away for the weekend and Hooey was sure that – in the interests of safety – they wouldn't mind him rearranging their children's garden play equipment. Twig stood nervously at the top of the plastic slide with his hands on his hips, looking down at Mrs Pinkerton's outdoor Jacuzzi. From the waist up he still looked very much like Twig. But his yellow tracksuit trousers had been stuffed with bubble wrap and, from the waist down, he now looked like the bottom half of a very large lemon.

"OK," said Hooey. "By recreating an unfortunate fairground incident, we'll be able to see how much protection the trousers offer." He looked at the slide and the Jacuzzi. "It's supposed to be a log flume. Obviously you'll need to use your imagination a bit."

"I am using my imagination," said Twig. "I'm imagining myself in an ambulance on the way to hospital."

"Positive thinking, Twig," said Hooey. "That's what we need."

"Do people fall out of log flumes a lot?" asked Twig.

"Safety's all about preparation," said Hooey, "and if somebody *did* fall out of a log flume, you can bet the first thing they'd say would be: Thank goodness for my TremTroos."

"Probably not the first thing," said Twig.

"They'd probably go: ARGGGHH! first."

"Well whatever. But at some point I'm sure they'd be grateful." Hooey opened his camera phone and got Twig in the centre of the picture. "Smile, Twig. You're the new Face of TremTroos."

Twig smiled and waved. "Shweet."

"OK, down to business," said Hooey when he'd taken the picture. "Skateboard?"

Twig unhooked the skateboard from the rungs of the ladder and held it up. "Check."

Hooey threw him the flowery pink cushion he had borrowed from Grandma. "Crash helmet?"

"Check," said Twig, securing it to his head with an elastic band.

"TremTroos fully bubble-wrapped?"

Twig punched himself in the leg and nodded. "Check."

"OK, Twig, let's run through it one more time. You're on a log flume at the fair, possibly with your family."

"**Oooh**, this is so enjoyable and lovely!" cried Twig happily.

"Good. That's the idea," said Hooey.

"When we've finished I'm going to buy you all an ice cream!"

"OK, Twig, that's very convincing, but now you need to focus because we're going to do the test."

"What test?"

"You know. Something goes wrong and you fall *out* of the log flume."

"Oh no!" said Twig. "What about my family?"

"There *is* no family."

"But I promised to buy them an ice cream."

"Twig, they're not real, remember? We're just *imagining* this."

"Oh right. Sorry."

Twig sat on the skateboard and clutched the handrail at the top of the slide. "Oh no everyone," he said to his imaginary family. "There's a problem with the log flume. I think there's been some kind of malfunction…"

"Wait for it," said Hooey, holding up his phone. "I'll say three, two, one *action* – and on *action* just push yourself down the slide and act terrified in a log flume emergency kind of way. Then I'll do a close-up on your trousers to demonstrate how they saved your life."

"OK," said Twig. "Gotcha."

Hooey pointed his phone at Twig and lined him up on the screen. "OK. THREE …"

Twig tensed his muscles.

"TWO …"

Twig gritted his teeth.

"ONE …"

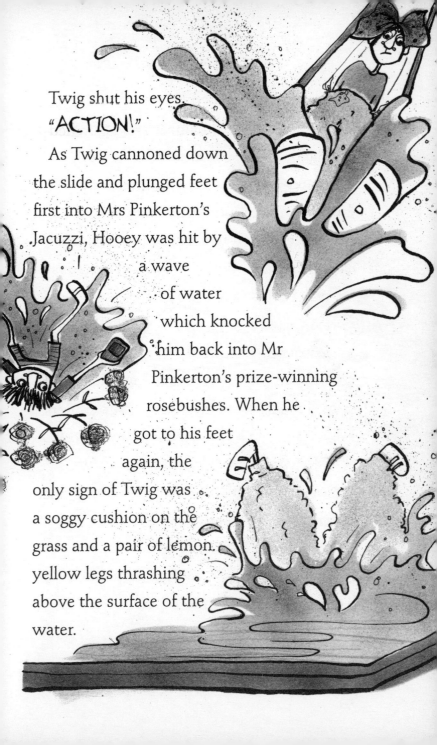

Twig shut his eyes.
"ACTION!"

As Twig cannoned down the slide and plunged feet first into Mrs Pinkerton's Jacuzzi, Hooey was hit by a wave of water which knocked him back into Mr Pinkerton's prize-winning rosebushes. When he got to his feet again, the only sign of Twig was a soggy cushion on the grass and a pair of lemon yellow legs thrashing above the surface of the water.

"That's good," called Hooey, zooming in on them with his camera. "Now come up so I can get a shot of your face."

There was silence for a moment and then Twig rose out of the water with a strangled cry before flapping over the side like a demented flounder fish. "TremTroos malfunction," he gasped.

ABORT! ABORT!

"That was excellent," said Hooey as Twig blew out a mouthful of water and rolled over onto his back. "Great acting, Twig!"

"I wasn't acting," said Twig. "Those trousers nearly killed me!"

"Shush, shush, shush!" said Hooey, hurriedly turning off his camera phone. "You have to stress the safety aspect. That's the whole point."

"Well I'm sorry," replied Twig, "but the whole point is that they tried to drown me. My head went down and my legs went up. If these trousers had their way, I'd still be down there now."

Hooey looked at Twig sitting in a puddle of water, bits of bubble wrap protruding from his trousers. "Maybe we should try it without the water," he said. "Just have you falling in some rosebushes or something."

"No way," said Twig, pulling off the trousers. "I've had enough pain for one day."

"But you're the Special Tester," said Hooey.

"Not any more," said Twig. "I quit."

"Hang on, Twig," said a voice. "Don't quit yet."

91

Hooey and Twig turned to see Will standing at the gate with a two-litre bottle of cola in each hand. He put down the bottles, pulled a roll of wallpaper from his blazer pocket and smiled.

"Just wait," he said, "until you see my plan."

TIGHTS AND
TOILETS

"Now then, now then!" shouted Miss
Troutson, clapping her hands together. "Our
very special Health and Safety assembly is
only ten minutes away, and we don't want
to keep the rest of the school waiting. So
make sure your presentations are ready and
don't forget to bring everything with you."

"Um, Miss Troutson," said Hooey when the other children had scurried away to their desks. "Can I go and help Twig get ready?"

Miss Troutson peered at him over the top of her glasses. "Whatever do you mean, child?"

"He's in the toilets undergoing some technical adjustments."

"Technical adjustments?"

"Yes. Will's doing it."

"Ah yes, *your brother*," said Miss Troutson, seeming to relax when she heard Will's name. "A sensible, hard-working boy. Well run along then. But make sure you're in the hall by quarter past ten."

"Yes Miss Troutson," said Hooey.

His fingers tingled with excitement as he thought about Will's latest plan. It was a brilliant idea, no doubt about it, and as he walked along the corridor he imagined himself standing in front of the whole school as they clapped and cheered and threw flowers at his feet. *"It was really nothing,"* he would say, catching a posy of flowers and bowing modestly. *"I couldn't have done it without my brother Will or my brave friend Twig."*

He imagined being carried out of assembly on people's shoulders, everyone shouting, *"Three cheers for Hooey! Three cheers for—"*

"HOOEY, where have you been?" said Will, sticking his head round the door of the boys' toilets. "We've been waiting ages."

"Sorry," said Hooey, his dream dissolving in a whiff of disinfectant. "Had to get permission from the Big Fish."

He followed Will into the toilets and saw that Twig was standing by the cubicles wearing nothing but a T-shirt and a pair of tights.

Hooey grinned. "You look nice."

"Don't, Hooey. I mean it," said Twig. He made a little space between his finger and thumb. "I am *this* far from quitting."

"OK, sorry," said Hooey, holding up his hands. He turned to Will. "Where are the TremTroos?"

"In there," replied Will, gesturing towards one of the cubicles. "Hanging up next to the dress."

"The *dress*?" said Twig, a look of horror on his face. "No one said anything about a dress!"

"Don't worry," said Hooey. "It's just to hide the TremTroos until the last moment. We borrowed a wig from Mrs Jenkins and we're going to introduce you as Mrs Twiggleton."

"Right, that's it," said Twig, peeling off his tights. "I'm out of here."

"Wait," said Hooey. "If you do this, you could go down as the first person to wear TremTroos in the whole of history. Ever."

"I don't care."

"Samantha will though."

Twig stopped, tights wrinkled round his knees. "What?"

"I told Samantha you were going to surprise everyone in assembly, and she said, 'Wow. Twig's so *cool.*'"

Twig's eyes widened. "Samantha said that?"

"Sure did. Think about it, Twig. In ten minutes' time, you could be the coolest kid in school."

Twig smiled. "Well if you put it like that…"

He bent over and began tugging up his tights again.

Will sighed and picked up the two bottles

of cola. "Hooey, help me shove these down his tights, will you?"

Twig pulled his tights open and Hooey pushed one bottle down his left leg with the neck pointing upwards.

"Steady," said Twig nervously as Will shoved the other one down his right leg. "I don't want to explode."

"Relax," said Hooey, twisting the cap of the bottle until it hissed. "These bad boys will only go off on your say-so."

The toilet door squeaked open and a small, blond-haired infant stood in the doorway, holding a plastic cup and hiccuping softly. His eyes widened as he stared at the scene before him.

"What's up?" said Twig. "Haven't you ever seen a girl with fizzy drinks down her tights before?"

The small boy shook his head and hiccuped some more.

"Well that's why you come to school," said Will as Hooey filled the boy's cup with water and gave it back to him. "It's called an education."

"There's a lesson he won't forget in a hurry," said Hooey as the sound of tiny hiccups faded up the corridor. "Dress to Impress, by Mrs Twiggleton."

"Look, can we just get on with this before he brings his whole class back for a guided tour?" said Twig irritably.

"OK, fine," said Will. "Balloons?"

"Balloons," said Hooey, producing two from his pocket. They were the long thin ones with knobbly bits up the sides.

"Perfect," said Will. "Mints?"

"You've got them, remember?"

"Oh yeah." Will rummaged around in his bag for a few seconds before pulling out two packets of chewy mints.

"Mints?" said Twig, frowning. "What are they for?"

"Not just *any* old mints," said Hooey as Will held them out like magic wands. "These are the secret ingredient of our all-new **Super TremTroos.**"

"Really?" said Twig. "*Super* TremTroos?"

"Yeah, but you need to be careful," said Will, opening the mints and pushing them into one of the balloons. "These things are super-powerful."

"What you have to do," said Hooey, dropping sweets into the other balloon, "is make sure you only drop in *one mint at a time.*"

"I don't understand," said Twig. "Drop it where?"

"In here," said Hooey, unscrewing the cola bottle cap and pushing the neck of the balloon over the end.

"Here's how it works," said Will. He unrolled a piece of wallpaper and Blu-Tacked

it to the mirror. "This is you," he said, using
his ruler to point to a smiling stick figure
with big ears. "And these are
the bottles in your tights."

"With you so far," said
Twig.

"Now, the balloons – *here*
– are full of mints, right?"

"Right."

"So it's important that
you keep your hands in your
pockets and squeeze the
balloons until you're ready
to activate the trousers."

"Why?"

"Because when you let go, the mints will
fall in the cola and make a gas which will
blow the balloons up in a safe and healthy
way, thus protecting you from the world
and all its dangers."

"The only slight, teensy-*weensy* problem," said Hooey, "is that we haven't had a chance to test it yet."

Twig chewed the side of his thumb nervously. "Is that bad?"

"Not *bad* exactly. It's just that Will only had enough money for two bottles of cola, so we don't know exactly how many chewy mints to use. But as long as you only drop in one at a time, you'll be fine. Won't he, Will?"

"Absolutely," said Will, slipping elastic bands over the neck of the balloons. "Just remember to take these off before you go in and hold onto the mints until you're ready. OK?"

"OK," said Twig.

Hooey heard the chatter of children making their way towards the hall and allowed himself to think about the moment when the free tickets to the fair would finally be theirs.

"Twig," he said, sliding his mum's make-up bag along the floor, "put your dress on and make yourself pretty. We've got a competition to win!"

TWIG TAKES OFF

"GOOD MORNING EVERYONE," said
Mr Croft, the headteacher.

"GOOD MORNING EVERYBODY!"
chorused two hundred and twenty-three
children.

Meanwhile, the two hundred and twenty-
fourth looked at himself in the mirror and
saw a strange woman called Mrs Twiggleton
staring back at him. "What to choose, what
to choose?" he said, reaching for the eye
shadow. "Flutter Me Beautiful or
Hello Pussy-cat?"

Back in the hall, Hooey sat cross-legged on the end of the row, waiting for the presentations to begin.

"Now then," continued Mr Croft, "Miss Troutson's class has been working on a project called **STAYING HEALTHY, STAYING SAFE**. So this morning we have a very special assembly in which the children will share some of the things they have been doing."

Miss Troutson nodded encouragingly and Hooey led the line of children to the front of the hall where they stood clutching bits of paper, paintings and junk models. As Ricky Mears stepped forward, the front row of infants all put their thumbs up.

"All right, Rick?" called a little boy with a shaven head. "You coming out later?"

Ricky was about to reply when the infant teacher put on her stern face and went *shush, shush, shush!* while Miss Troutson glared at

Ricky and hissed, *"Get on with it!"*

Ricky cleared his throat, held up his piece of paper and said in a loud voice, "We have been learning how to be Healthy. We have been learning how to be Safe. This is the things what we have been learning."

As Miss Troutson smiled and mouthed *Well done* at him, Basbo stepped forward and held up several pieces of wood that had been roughly nailed together in the shape of a club.

"The world's a dangerous place, innit," he said. "If you get attacked by tigers or dinosaurs, you're gonna need to get yourself one of these."

"YAY!" shouted the infants.

Bazzer waved his club at them and made caveman noises:

UG-UG-UG-UG-EURGGGH!

The infants shrieked happily, clutching their heads and falling backwards into the row behind.

"No, no, *NO!*" shouted Miss Troutson, striding up to the front and snatching Basbo's club away. She turned to the headteacher and smiled thinly. "Sorry about that," she said. "I think Barry must have got a little bit confused."

She put the club behind the piano and nudged Basbo with her elbow. "Show them your poster," she hissed.

Sulkily, Basbo held up a poster which said:

STAY SAFE
DON'T GO OUT

"Hmmm," said the headteacher. "Interesting."

"It was all a bit last-minute," explained Miss Troutson apologetically. "But I actually think Barry has worked extremely hard on his drawing."

Basbo's picture showed someone peering out through a window. They were dressed in what appeared to be a suit of armour with wire coming out of it. The end of the wire was plugged into the mains.

"Iss electric," said Basbo. "Anyone touches you and KER-BAM! End of story."

"Right, thank you Barry," said Miss Troutson hurriedly. She turned to Sarah-Jane Silverton. "Sarah-Jane, perhaps you'd like to tell everyone about *your* idea?"

"Certainly, Miss Troutson," said Sarah-Jane. "It would be my pleasure."

She reached down and picked up a shoebox which she had painted red and gold. As the morning sunlight streamed through the windows, it sparkled and shone like a gift from heaven.

"**Ooooh!**" went the infants.

Uh-oh, thought Hooey. *Serious competition.*

"This may look like an ordinary shoebox," said Sarah-Jane in her tinkly, musical voice, "but inside is a special lesson for us all on how to be healthy *and* safe."

She released a tiny silver catch on the edge of the box and the side dropped down to reveal a miniature doll's house. Everyone in the hall gasped as Sarah-Jane held it up to show the tiny furniture hidden inside. A little family of dolls was seated at the table, enjoying a small but healthy supper.

Hooey looked across and saw that Mr Croft actually had tears in his eyes. His hands were clasped to his chest and he appeared to be whispering the words *so* and *beautiful* over and over again.

Will was looking worried. As Sarah-Jane said, "I would now like to take you on a short tour of Dolly's World, pointing out matters of Health and Safety along the way…" Hooey sidled over to Miss Troutson and whispered, *"Miss, I need to get Twig. He's still in the toilets."*

"What?" Miss Troutson frowned. "Why?"

"He's getting ready."

"Oh, run along then," said Miss Troutson, anxious not to miss any more of Sarah-Jane's presentation. "But hurry up. You're on next."

When Hooey got to the toilets, Twig was still putting on his make-up.

"I wasn't sure which lipstick to go for," he said. "In the end I went for *Kiss Me Pink*." He smacked his lips against a paper towel and looked in the mirror. "What d'you think? Too much?"

"Never mind all that," said Hooey. "Grab your mints and release the bands. We're on next."

*   *   *

Back in the hall, Sarah-Jane was coming
to the end of her presentation. "And that's
why," she was saying, "it's important to be
Healthy *and* Safe ..." picking up the tiniest
doll, she paused for effect, smiled at the
infants and added, "how*ever* small you are!"

"BRAVO!" shouted Mr Croft as the staff
rose from their seats to applaud. "BRAVO!"

"OK," said Hooey as they waited outside
the hall doors. "Things aren't looking great.
But if you
play it cool
and don't
inflate your
trousers too
early, we're
still in with
a chance."

As Sarah-Jane went back to her place, Hooey walked to the front of the hall and stood with his hands on his hips, waiting for silence.

"Keeping dolls healthy and safe is one thing," he said when everyone had quietened down. "But what happens if you're not a doll? What then? *Hmm?*"

All around the room, teachers turned to one another and nodded, recognizing that Hooey had asked an important question.

"I'll tell you what then," Hooey continued, "that's the time to get yourself some EXTRA SPECIAL PROTECTION. Ladies and gentlemen, please put your hands together for …

... MRS TWIGGLETON!"

The door swung open and Twig appeared, his lilac dress swishing as he flounced down the side of the hall.

Miss Troutson peered over the top of her glasses as if she couldn't quite believe what she was seeing. Everyone else pointed and chattered excitedly until Hooey held up his hands again for quiet.

"OK," said Hooey. "Mrs Twiggleton will now demonstrate an amazing new invention which could save your life. Isn't that right, Mrs Twiggleton?"

"That's right. dear," said Twig in a high, squeaky voice. "Safety first."

"Bless her," said Hooey. "She's *so* brave. Samantha, if you wouldn't mind?"

Samantha Curbitt stepped forward and placed a leather football on the floor.

"Now we all know that football can be fun," said Hooey. "But imagine if Mrs Twiggleton was standing behind the goal and someone missed a penalty. What would happen *then*?"

Will immediately put his hand up and Hooey pointed to him. "Yes Will?"

"I imagine, Hooey, that she would be in a great deal of DANGER."

"He's right, ladies and gentlemen," said Hooey. "At least, *normally* she would. But underneath this dress, Mrs Twiggleton is wearing something which will offer her maximum protection. Underneath this dress, Mrs Twiggleton is wearing a pair of SUPER TREMTROOS!"

Hooey was about to
signal for Twig to release a
couple of the mints when he saw Samantha
walk backwards and start to take a run-up.

He just had time to shout, "**NOT YET,
SAMA—**" before she blammed the ball as
hard as she could into Twig's lower portions.

Twig flew backwards
and crashed into
the music trolley,
sending chime
bars flying in all
directions.

"Oh good grief!"
cried the headteacher.
"Are you all right, Mrs
Twiggleton?"

Twig staggered to his feet and gave a
lopsided smile. "I'm fine!" he squeaked. "And
it's all thanks to my TremTroos!"

There was a loud cheer and, just for a few seconds, Hooey thought they might actually be in with a chance of winning. But as Twig put his thumbs up, Hooey heard the faint rattle of mints, followed by a plopping sound. There was a loud fizzing, and then Twig's dress slowly began to swell up like some strange, bloated jellyfish.

"Uh-oh," said Twig.

The infants gasped.

Miss Troutson crossed herself.

Then, as the huge, cola-filled balloons began lifting the bottom of Twig's skirt, Mr Croft started to run for the doors, shouting, "TAKE COVER, EVERYONE! I THINK MRS TWIGGLETON'S GONNA BLOW!"

124

But he was too late.

With a noise that could be heard in the chip shop three miles away, Twig's trousers exploded, drenching the whole room with a soggy mixture of diet cola and chewy mints.

Outside, Mr Bilks the caretaker watched in horror as the hall windows suddenly turned brown, as if a vat of gravy had exploded inside a microwave.

Back in the hall, Hooey opened his eyes to see the front four rows of children sitting in stunned silence, their hair blown backwards by the force of the blast.

Miss Troutson sat in her chair with her mouth open, diet cola dripping from the end of her nose. And at the back of the hall, Mr Croft stood with one hand still reaching for the door, the outline of his body imprinted on the wall behind him.

At that moment, Twig appeared in the doorway to the PE cupboard with his clothes in shreds. "Has anyone seen my trousers?" he asked. Then he fell back into the cupboard again.

"**HOOEY HIGGINS**," said Miss Troutson, standing up and folding her arms as a sticky pool of cola began to form around her shoes. "Was this *your* idea, by any chance?"

Hooey nodded. "Yes it was. But I've got some better ones."

He smiled hopefully.

"Do you want to hear them?"

SANDERSON'S SURPRISE

"Never mind, love," said Hooey's mum as the family sat down for dinner. "You did your best, which is all that matters."

Hooey shook his head. "That's not what Miss Troutson said. She said what matters is not blowing your trousers up in assembly."

Will nodded. "She was actually very clear on that point."

"So what went wrong then?" asked Dad, helping himself to some potatoes.

"Twig used too many mints," said Will. "I told him not to, but he just went ahead and bunged the whole lot in."

"To be fair," said Hooey, "I think he lost concentration when Samantha's football whacked him in the you-know-wheres."

"That's why I always lose to your grandma at tennis on the Nintendo Wii," said Grandpa.

"It's your own fault," said Grandma. "You stand too close when I'm serving."

There was a loud knock at the door and Grandpa pushed his chair back. "I'll get it," he said, winking at Hooey. "I don't want to stand too close to Grandma while she's serving."

Hooey rested his chin on the palm of his hand and watched Grandma dish up the vegetables. He'd been so sure that the

TremTroos would win the competition.
He'd imagined celebrating at the fair with
Twig and Will, going on all the free rides and
having a crazy time.

But instead the prize had gone to
Sarah-Jane Silverton and her Dollies from
Dullsville. Hooey guessed she'd probably
just take them for a quick ride on the
teacups and go straight home again.

He sighed.

All that work.

All that work for nothing…

"Hooey," called Grandpa.

"There's someone at the door
to see you."

"Me?"

"Yes, it's a Mr
Sanderson. Says he
wants to talk to you
about his son."

Pushing his plate to one side, Hooey walked out into the hallway and was alarmed to find a very large man standing at the door with his arms folded. He wore big clumpy boots and his arms were covered with tattoos of anchors and swords with fierce-looking snakes wrapped around them.

"Um, hello," said Hooey nervously. "Can I help?"

"That depends," said the man gruffly. "Are you Hooey Higgins?"

Hooey nodded.

"And are you the person responsible for the exploding trousers?"

"Which ones?" asked Hooey, hoping the man had got him mixed up with some other exploding trouser incident.

"The ones at school."

Hooey's face fell. "I'm afraid so," he said.

The man leaned on the doorframe. "You do realize," he said, "that you scared the living daylights out of my son Sammy today?"

"I'm sorry," said Hooey, trying to remember if he knew anyone called Sammy Sanderson. "But I don't think…"

"He said there were three of you," said the man. "Is that right?"

As he already seemed to know all the details, Hooey guessed there was no point in denying it. "Yes," he said. "But I can't give you their names."

"Twig and Will, wasn't it?"

"Yep, that's them."

Hooey was just wondering if he could make a run for it when he looked up and saw, to his surprise, that the man had a huge smile on his face.

"Well I just came round to say thanks," he said.

"**Eh?**" said Hooey.

"You have no idea what it's been like these past few weeks," the man continued. "Morning, noon and night, on and on and on, driving the whole family nuts."

"**Eh?**" said Hooey again.

"My son Sammy. Three weeks we've had to put up with his blinkin' hiccups. Three weeks! But then you come along, blow your trousers up and that's it, job done. Cured him in an instant!"

It was then that Hooey remembered the small boy in the toilets. "So you're not cross then?"

"Cross?" replied the man. "I'm over the moon, my son! And just to prove it, I've brought you something to say thanks."

He pulled an envelope from his back

pocket and handed it to Hooey. "It's not much, but it's the least I can do. Anyway, thanks again, mate."

Hooey watched him go and then walked back into the dining room with the envelope in his hand.

"Who was that?" asked Will. "He looked a bit scary."

"He was nice actually," said Hooey. "Just came to say thanks for blowing up Grandma's trousers."

"I must be getting old," said Grandma, peering down at her nylon slacks. "I didn't even notice."

"You know who he is, don't you?" said Dad.

"Sammy Sanderson's dad apparently," said Hooey.

"Well yes. But he also happens to own the fairground." Dad smiled and picked up a serving dish. "More peas, anyone?"

Hooey stared at the envelope in his hand.

"Will," he said, "get me the phone."

Twig was in his bedroom
when the phone rang.

"Hello?" he said. "Twig's
residence."

As he listened to what Hooey
had to say, Twig stared out of the
window and watched the coloured lights
of the fair flickering on in the distance.

"Go on then," he said nervously. "Open it."

Back at Hooey's house, everyone fell silent
as Hooey tore open the envelope.

"Well?" whispered Twig. "Is it what you
thought it was?"

Hooey peered inside the
envelope and grinned.

"You'd better believe it, Twiggy-boy," he said, pulling out the contents and waving them in the air. "We've done it! **WE'VE GOT THREE FREE TICKETS TO THE FAIR!**"

Then as Will jumped out of his chair and Dingbat began barking excitedly, Hooey took the phone from his ear and held it up so that everyone could hear the sound of Twig dancing around his bedroom, cheering and yelling and shouting at the top of his voice…

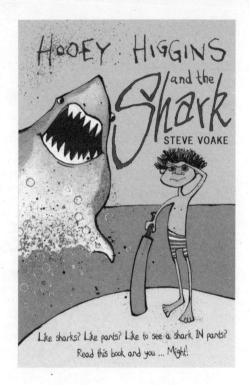